The World God Made

by Donna D. Cooner, Ed.D. illus. by Kim Simons

WORD
Kids!

WORD PUBLISHING
Dallas·London·Vancouver·Melbourne

To William and Anna who laid the foundation.
—DDC

For Chloe.
—KS

The World God Made

Managing Editor: Laura Minchew
Project Editor: Brenda Ward

Scripture taken from the HOLY BIBLE, NEW INTERNATIONAL VERSION.
Copyright © 1973, 1978, 1984 International Bible Society.
Used by permission of Zondervan Bible Publishers.

Library of Congress Cataloging-in-Publication Data.

Cooner, Donna D. (Donna Danell)
  The world God made/by Donna Conner; illustrated by Kim Simons.
    p. cm.
  "Word kids!"
      Summary: In the style of "The House That Jack Built," describes God's
  creations, followed by a prayer of thanks.
      ISBN 0–8499–1162–1
      [1. Creation—Fiction. 2. Nature—Fiction. 3. Stories in rhyme.]
  I. Simons, Kim, 1955– ill. II. Title.
  PZ8.3.C779Wo 1994
  [E]—dc20
                                                        94–3333
                                                          CIP
                                                          AC

Printed in the United States of America
4 5 6 7 8 9   L B M   9 8 7 6 5 4 3 2

This is the world
that God made.

This is the light
that shines on the world
that God made.

This is the sky
that's touched with the light
that shines on the world
that God made.

This is the field
that's under the sky
that's touched with the light
that shines on the world
that God made.

This is the stream
that runs through the field
that's under the sky
that's touched with the light
that shines on the world
that God made.

This is the tree
that grows by the stream
that runs through the field
that's under the sky
that's touched with the light
that shines on the world
that God made.

This is the cat
that climbs down the tree
that grows by the stream
that runs through the field
that's under the sky
that's touched with the light
that shines on the world
that God made.

This is the dog
that chases the cat
that climbs down the tree
that grows by the stream
that runs through the field
that's under the sky
that's touched with the light
that shines on the world
that God made.

This is the boy
that calls to the dog
that chases the cat
that climbs down the tree
that grows by the stream
that runs through the field
that's under the sky
that's touched with the light
that shines on the world
that God made.

Thank you, God, for the dog, quiet and good.
Thank you, God, for the cat, furry and small.

Thank you, God, for the tree, strong and tall.

Thank you, God, for the stream, cool and clear.

Thank you, God, for the field, grassy and near.

Thank you, God, for the sky, pink and gray.

Thank you, God, for the light's fading rays.

Thank you, God, for the world you made.

"God saw all that he had made, and it was very good."

Genesis 1:31